GOSCINNY AND UDERZO
PRESENT
An Asterix Adventure

ASTERIX
IN
CORSICA

Written by RENÉ GOSCINNY *and Illustrated by* ALBERT UDERZO

Translated by Anthea Bell *and* Derek Hockridge

ORION

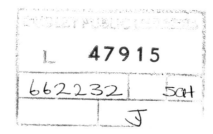
Original title: *Astérix en Corse*

Exclusive Licensee: Orion Publishing Group
Translators: Anthea Bell and Derek Hockridge
Typography: Bryony Newhouse

This revised edition first published in 2004 by
Orion Books Ltd
Orion House, 5 Upper St Martin's Lane
London WC2H 9EA

Printed in France by Partenaires

http://gb.asterix.com
www.orionbooks.co.uk

A CIP catalogue record for this book is available from the British Library

ISBN 0752866435 (cased)
ISBN 0752866443 (paperback)

Distributed in the United States of America by Sterling Publishing Co. Inc.
387 Park Avenue South, New York, NY 10016

FACTOTUM

GERANIUM

PENDULUM

POSTSCRIPTUM

AXIUM

DELPHINIUM

RADIUM

HUM

ULTIMATUM

VANITASVANITATUM

AUDITORIUM

MAUSOLEUM

PODIUM

PREMIUM

ALERIA

HARMONIUM

MARIANA

OPIUM

PANDEMONIUM

EUPHONIUM

BUNKUM

CHEWINGUM

WELCUM

CREMATORIUM

ALBUM

CALCIUM

TEDIUM

MODICUM

AGYLLA

INDECORUM

ADDENDUM

HUMDRUM

VADEMECUM

OPOSSUM

MEMORANDUM

MAXIMUM

POTASSIUM

MINIMUM

ALUMINIUM

CHRYSANTHEMUM

QUODERATDEMONSTRANDUM
(WEST)

DESIDERATUM

STERNUM

**PORTUS
SYRACUSANUS**

ADINFINITUM

QUODERATDEMONSTRANDUM
(EAST)

REFERENDUM

SODIUM

TOWNS

FORTIFIED
ROMAN CAMPS

STRONTIUM

SAECULASAECULORUM

ASTERIX, THE HERO OF THESE ADVENTURES. A SHREWD, CUNNING LITTLE WARRIOR, ALL PERILOUS MISSIONS ARE IMMEDIATELY ENTRUSTED TO HIM. ASTERIX GETS HIS SUPERHUMAN STRENGTH FROM THE MAGIC POTION BREWED BY THE DRUID GETAFIX . . .

OBELIX, ASTERIX'S INSEPARABLE FRIEND. A MENHIR DELIVERY MAN BY TRADE, ADDICTED TO WILD BOAR. OBELIX IS ALWAYS READY TO DROP EVERYTHING AND GO OFF ON A NEW ADVENTURE WITH ASTERIX – SO LONG AS THERE'S WILD BOAR TO EAT, AND PLENTY OF FIGHTING. HIS CONSTANT COMPANION IS DOGMATIX, THE ONLY KNOWN CANINE ECOLOGIST, WHO HOWLS WITH DESPAIR WHEN A TREE IS CUT DOWN.

GETAFIX, THE VENERABLE VILLAGE DRUID, GATHERS MISTLETOE AND BREWS MAGIC POTIONS. HIS SPECIALITY IS THE POTION WHICH GIVES THE DRINKER SUPERHUMAN STRENGTH. BUT GETAFIX ALSO HAS OTHER RECIPES UP HIS SLEEVE . . .

CACOFONIX, THE BARD. OPINION IS DIVIDED AS TO HIS MUSICAL GIFTS. CACOFONIX THINKS HE'S A GENIUS. EVERYONE ELSE THINKS HE'S UNSPEAKABLE. BUT SO LONG AS HE DOESN'T SPEAK, LET ALONE SING, EVERYBODY LIKES HIM . . .

FINALLY, VITALSTATISTIX, THE CHIEF OF THE TRIBE. MAJESTIC, BRAVE AND HOT-TEMPERED, THE OLD WARRIOR IS RESPECTED BY HIS MEN AND FEARED BY HIS ENEMIES. VITALSTATISTIX HIMSELF HAS ONLY ONE FEAR, HE IS AFRAID THE SKY MAY FALL ON HIS HEAD TOMORROW. BUT AS HE ALWAYS SAYS, TOMORROW NEVER COMES.

I'M GOING TO TELL MY DADDY AND YOU'LL BE THORRY, THO THERE!

DO WE NEED TO LAY A PLACE FOR CACOFONIX THE BARD?

YES, EVERYONE CELEBRATES THE ANNIVERSARY OF THE GAULS' VICTORY AT GERGOVIA, EVEN THE BARD.

AND DON'T FORGET, THIS YEAR'S ANNIVERSARY CELEBRATIONS ARE VERY SPECIAL! WE'VE INVITED ALL OUR FRIENDS WHO HAVE FOUGHT WELL AGAINST THE ROMANS TOO. I WANT EVERYTHING IN THIS VILLAGE PERFECT TO RECEIVE THEM, STARTING WITH YOU!

HEAR THAT, YOU TWO?

IT WAS HIS BRAT TOLD MY BOY I SOLD ROTTEN...

WHO WERE YOU CALLING A BRAT?

STOP IT!

I WANT EVERYTHING SPOTLESSLY CLEAN! INCLUDING MY SHIELD ...IT'S FILTHY! JUST LOOK AT IT!

WHAT, NOW?

IT'S NOT ALL THAT DIRTY...

I CAN'T SEE ANYTHING...

SOMETIMES I WONDER IF IT'S ALL WORTH WHILE...

IN THE FORTIFIED ROMAN CAMP OF TOTORUM...

RIGHT! EVERYONE READY?

AND ABOUT TIME TOO! FORWARD MARCH... AND IN SILENCE, PLEASE.

I'M ON A MISSION, CENTURION. WE'VE COME A LONG WAY. I WANT SHELTER FOR THE NIGHT BEFORE WE CONTINUE OUR JOURNEY.

THE FACT IS... WE WERE JUST GOING OUT.

BONG!

HOW MANY OF YOU? WHERE?

ER... ALL OF US. GOING ON MANOEUVRES IN THE HINTERLAND.

YOU MEAN YOU'RE LEAVING THE CAMP UNGUARDED?

ER... SORT OF...

ARE WE OFF, CENTURION?

WHAT ARE WE WAITING FOR, BY JUPITER?

TIME'S GETTING ON!

WELL, I'M AWFULLY SORRY AND ALL THAT... DROP US A SLAB IN ADVANCE ANOTHER TIME. AVE. WE'RE OFF.

NO ONE'S OFF ANYWHERE!

I AM ON A SPECIAL MISSION FROM PRAETOR PERFIDIUS, GOVERNOR OF CORSICA, AND I DEMAND AN EXPLANATION OF THIS SUSPICIOUS HASTE!

LISTEN, CENTURION HIPPOPOTAMUS, IF YOU DON'T MIND WE'LL GO ON AHEAD AND YOU JOIN US LATER, ALL RIGHT?

NO, IT IS NOT ALL RIGHT!

7

HERE, COME INTO MY TENT... DON'T START WITHOUT ME, YOU LOT. THIS WON'T TAKE LONG.

?

TODAY IS THE ANNIVERSARY OF THE BATTLE OF GERGOVIA. THE PEOPLE OF THE NEARBY GAULISH VILLAGE HAVE A WAY OF CELEBRATING THE OCCASION BY ATTACKING THE NEIGHBOURING ROMAN GARRISONS.

AND YOU DON'T ATTEMPT TO STOP THIS LOCAL CUSTOM?

WE CERTAINLY DO! WE STOP IT BY LEAVING CAMP AND GOING ON MANOEUVRES!

ARE YOU READY, CENTURION HIPPOPOTAMUS? THE BOYS ARE GETTING A BIT IMPATIENT, AND...

ARE THESE GAULS REALLY SO FEROCIOUS?

WELL, TOO BAD. I'M ESCORTING A CORSICAN EXILE, AND HE'S SPENDING THE NIGHT IN THIS CAMP. YOU AND YOUR GARRISON ARE RESPONSIBLE TO CAESAR FOR HIS SAFE KEEPING. I'LL BE BACK TO PICK HIM UP TOMORROW.

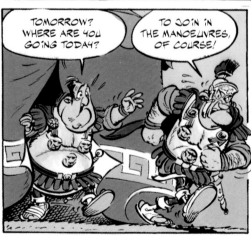

TOMORROW? WHERE ARE YOU GOING TODAY?

TO JOIN IN THE MANOEUVRES, OF COURSE!

BUT... BUT YOU CAN'T DO THIS TO US! THE GAULS WILL SLAUGHTER US! WHAT'S MORE, IF THEY SEE WE'VE GOT A PRISONER HERE, THEY'LL...

BRING THE EXILE ALONG!

AVE, CENTURION, AND DON'T FORGET, CAESAR WILL HOLD YOU RESPONSIBLE!

THE FIRST GUESTS ARE ARRIVING AT THE LITTLE GAULISH VILLAGE...

PETITSUIX!

I'VE BROUGHT YOU A HELVETIAN CHEESE.

HUEVOS Y BACON!

OLÉ, HOMBRES, OLÉ!

DOGMATIX!

INSTANTMIX! YOU'VE COME ALL THE WAY FROM ROME!

I JUST HAD TO HEAR THE SOUND OF YOUR VOICE AGAIN!

ANTICLIMAX! MYKINGDOMFORANOS! O'VEROPTIMISTIX! McANIX! DIPSOMANIAX!

I SAY, OLD BOY, THIS IS SIMPLY MARVELLOUS, WHAT? GOOD TO SEE YOU, COUSIN ASTERIX!

JELLIBABIX FROM LUGDUNUM! DRINKLIKAFIX FROM MASSILIA! SENIORSERVIX FROM GESOCRIBATUM!

WINESANSPIRIX THE ARVERNIAN!

REMEMBER HOW WE DIDDLED CAESAR OUT OF THE CHIEFTAIN'S SHIELD?

WHAT A PRETTY DRESS!

YES, IT'S MADE OF OUR OWN LUGDUNUM * SILK.

* LYONS

I'M ENJOYING BEING LIONISED LIKE THIS TOO.

HOMBRE! I USE OLIVE OIL FOR ALL MY COOKING!

YOU DON'T SAY! FANCY THAT! I USE BOILING WATER. IT GIVES EVERYTHING A LOVELY FLAVOUR, DON'T YOU KNOW?

REMEMBER HOW WE BOWLED THOSE ROMANS OVER IN MASSILIA?

HAHAHAHA!

REMEMBER WHEN YOU WERE EATING HOLES IN CHEESE IN THAT GENEVA BANK VAULT?

AN ARMED VIGIL IS IN PROGRESS AT TOTORUM...

...AND THERE'LL BE THE GREAT BIG BRUTE, AND THE DREADFUL LITTLE MIDGET, ALL STUFFED WITH MAGIC POTION, AND THEY WON'T LIKE IT WHEN THEY SEE WE'VE GOT A PRISONER EITHER...

CHATTER CHATTER CHATTER

CHATTER CHATTER CHATTER CHATTER

OH NO, BY JUPITER! THIS IS TOO MUCH!

CHATTER CHATTER

LISTEN, I'M GOING TO UNLOCK YOUR CHAINS...

IF THEY RECAPTURE YOU, YOU MUST PROMISE TO SAY YOU ESCAPED ON YOUR OWN AND NO ONE HELPED YOU... DON'T ASK WHY I'M DOING THIS FOR YOU...

CLICK!

8A

YOU CAN GO! YOU'RE FREE!

I SAID: YOU CAN GO! YOU'RE FREE!

LISTEN, WILL YOU? YOU'RE FREE! YOU CAN GO!

AFTER MY SIESTA.

WHAT DO YOU MEAN, AFTER YOUR SIESTA?

IT'S GETTING LATE, ROMAN. IF I DON'T HAVE MY SIESTA NOW, I SHAN'T HAVE TIME TO HAVE IT BEFORE BEDTIME, SO LEAVE ME ALONE OR I MIGHT LOSE MY TEMPER.

LOOK, ARE YOU OR ARE YOU NOT GOING TO ESCAPE?!

THEY'RE COMING, CENTURION HIPPOPOTAMUS, AND THEY'VE GOT SOME FRIENDS WITH THEM. WE WOULDN'T LIKE YOU TO MISS THE START.

8B

13

WHO ARE YOU? YOU'RE NOT A ROMAN!

GRRRAO!

CERTAINLY NOT. I'M AN EXILED PRISONER SLEEPING OVERNIGHT IN THIS CAMP. THOUGH I DON'T KNOW THAT MY ESCORTS HAVE PICKED THE RIGHT SPOT FOR A GOOD NIGHT'S REST.

A PRISONER?

YES, BUT YOU CAN'T DO ANYTHING ABOUT IT NOW! YOU'VE BASHED US UP ALREADY! TRICKED YOU THAT TIME, DIDN'T WE?

WHAT'S YOUR NAME? WHY WERE YOU EXILED?

MY NAME IS BONEYWASAWARRIORWAYAYIX, AND I COME FROM CORSICA.

WHAT'S CORSICA?

CORSICA IS THE ROMANS' BUGBEAR! GET THAT, FATTY?

I AM NOT FAT AND I'M THE ROMANS' BUGBEAR TOO!

YOU'RE TOUCHY... I LIKE YOU!

WELL, WELLINGTON WASA...

BONEY-WASA.

SORRY. WELL, BONEYWASAWARRIOR-WAYAYIX, COME TO OUR VILLAGE, SHARE OUR BANQUET...

...AND TELL US ALL ABOUT IT.

DOGMATIX, HEEL!

HARFHARFHARF!

14

DON'T YOU LIKE BOAR, BONEYWASAWARRIORWAYAYIX?

FUNNY, THAT MAN'S NAME INSPIRES ME. I'VE GOT AN IDEA FOR A SONG... MAYBE A SHANTY...

YES, I LIKE BOAR... BUT I CAN SEE YOU'RE JUST OFFERING IT TO ME OUT OF PITY.

NOT A BIT OF IT!

IF YOU DON'T WANT IT, I'LL TAKE IT OFF YOUR HANDS...

I HAVE UPSET YOU. YOU'RE PROUD AND TOUCHY. I LIKE YOU, LITTLE MAN.

VERY WELL, I'LL EAT THIS BOAR.

YOU'VE UPSET ME NOW ALL RIGHT!

TELL US ABOUT YOUR COUNTRY, BONEYWASA-WARRIORWAYAYIX.

CORSICA IS A ROMAN PROVINCE GOVERNED BY A PRAETOR APPOINTED ANNUALLY. DURING HIS YEAR IN OFFICE, THE PRAETOR RANSACKS CORSICA, CLAIMING TO BE LEVYING TAXES, BUT HE REALLY WANTS TO BE IN JULIUS CAESAR'S GOOD BOOKS WHEN HE RETURNS TO ROME.

FOR PITY'S SAKE, A BOAR!

BUT BEFORE THE PRAETOR LEAVES, I AND MY MEN GET BACK EVERYTHING HE HAD IN HIS WAREHOUSES. SO FAR CAESAR'S ONLY HAD PEANUTS OUT OF US... NOT EVEN ONE OF OUR CORSICAN CHESTNUTS.

THE PRESENT PRAETOR, PERFIDIUS, IS THE GREEDIEST AND CRUELLEST WE'VE HAD YET. AN ENEMY BETRAYED ME TO HIM AT SIESTA TIME, AND HE CONDEMNED ME TO THE WORST OF PUNISHMENTS: EXILE! BUT THANKS TO YOU, I SHALL BE BACK IN CORSICA BEFORE THE PRAETOR LEAVES, IN TIME TO GET BACK ALL THE LOOT HE'S STOLEN!

I'D BE INTERESTED TO SEE HOW YOU DEAL WITH THE ROMANS!

SCRUNCH! SCRUNCH! SCRUNCH!

WELL, WHY NOT COME WITH ME, ASTERIXOCELLIX? WHEN YOU GET HOME, YOU CAN TELL YOUR FRIENDS HOW WE DO THESE THINGS IN CORSICA, THE MOST BEAUTIFUL COUNTRY IN THE WORLD!

YES, BUT NOT JUST YET. I NEED A NAP FIRST.

COME TO MY ARMS, LITTLE MAN! YES, I REALLY DO LIKE YOU!

RIGHT, THAT'S SETTLED! TOMORROW MORNING ASTERIX AND OBELIX WILL LEAVE FOR CORSICA WITH YOU. WHEN THEY COME BACK THEY CAN TELL US WHAT METHODS YOU CORSICANS USE, AND WHAT YOUR COUNTRY'S LIKE!

NEXT MORNING...

I SAY, OLD FRUIT, YOU DO A GOOD LINE IN PARTIES!

YES, MARVELLOUS PARTY LINE!

SUCH LIBERALITY! OUR TASTES ARE CONSERVATIVE, BUT YOU DIDN'T LABOUR IN VAIN!

AND JUST WHY SHOULDN'T I TAKE HIM?

HERE WE GO AGAIN! BECAUSE HE'S TOO SMALL, THAT'S WHY!

WE'VE BEEN LOOKING FOR YOU EVERYWHERE, BOYS. YOU'D BETTER LEAVE BEFORE THE ROMANS COME BACK. DON'T FORGET, OUR CORSICAN FRIEND IS IN GREAT DEMAND.

GRUMBLE-GRUMBLE-GRUMBLE...

GNAGNAGNA GNAGNAGNA...

AND HERE'S A GOURD OF MAGIC POTION FOR YOU TOO, BONEYWASAWARRIORWAYAYIX. A USEFUL LITTLE GIFT AS A MEMENTO OF YOUR VISIT TO US.

JUST A MINUTE! I'VE GOT A USEFUL LITTLE GIFT FOR YOU TOO!

A LITTLE DOG! I'M VERY FOND OF LITTLE DOGS!

?

IT MEANS I CAN TRAVEL LIGHT, TOO. HE'LL HAVE TO CARRY DOGMATIX, AND DOGMATIX HAS BEEN PUTTING ON A BIT OF WEIGHT LATELY...

OH, VERY CLEVER, OBELIX!

YOU DON'T CATCH US BONY CHARACTERS NAPPING, ASTERIXOCELLIX!

16

THE PORT OF MASSILIA...

I MUST FIND A BOAT TO TAKE US TO CORSICA. I HAVE FRIENDS IN MASSILIA WHO'LL HELP ME, BUT I'D BETTER GO ON MY OWN.

WE'LL MEET HERE IN AN HOUR'S TIME. HOLD THIS DOG FOR ME, I'M RATHER TIRED.

VERMICELLIX

BONEYWASA-WARRIORWAYAYIX, I AM BESIDE MYSELF WITH JOY.

VERMICELLIX, THE SIGHT OF YOU FILLS ME WITH PLEASURE.

MORTADELLA, LET'S HAVE SOME WINE AND SOME SAUSAGE. NOT THE STUFF WE GIVE THE CUSTOMERS.

NOW, GO AND SEE TO THE CUSTOMERS.

MPH.

THIS SAUSAGE BRINGS BACK MEMORIES OF MY NATIVE LAND! SO FRESH YOU CAN ALMOST HEAR IT BRAYING.

STILL PRETTY, AS YOU CAN SEE, BUT SHE JUST CAN'T KEEP HER MOUTH SHUT. WELL, THAT'S ENOUGH ABOUT WOMEN. I THOUGHT YOU WERE IN EXILE?

NOT ANY MORE. YOU MUST FIND ME A BOAT TO CROSS BACK TO CORSICA.

CLICK!

IT WON'T BE EASY. THE ROMANS ARE WATCHING THE PORT. BUT I'VE GOT SOME SAILORS IN THERE WHO SEEM TO BE PRETTY COOL CUSTOMERS. COME ON.

ANYTHING ELSE YOU FANCY?

NOT A SAUSAGE, EH, CAP'N?

I'D LIKE TO MAKE YOU AN OFFER. WILL YOU TAKE SOME MEN ON BOARD FOR CORSICA? VERY DISCREETLY. NAME YOUR PRICE.

THE PRICE IS RIGHT, BUT THEY'LL NEED GOLD FOR SHIPBOARD EXPENSES.

SOON AFTERWARDS...

WELL, THAT'S FIXED. WE EMBARK TONIGHT. COME ON, I KNOW SOMEWHERE WE CAN HAVE A SIESTA.

TCHAC!

HEY, YOU!

?

SEE?

HARRGH HARRGH HARRGH! PASSENGERS, WITH LOTS OF GOLD. ONCE AT SEA, WE'LL CLEAN THEM OUT AND MAKE THEM WALK THE PLANK. NO MORE BOARDING SHIPS FOR US, WE'RE GOING IN FOR OVERBOARDING!

O TEMPORA, O MORES!

AND MORE'S THE WORD.

18

THAT NIGHT...

WHO GOES THERE?

CORSICAN, WITH FRIENDS. CAN HE COME ON BOARD?

'COURSE HE CAN.

SEEMS WE'RE ON THE RIGHT COURSE...

SO IT DOES.

YOUR CABIN IS BETWEEN DECKS. YOU CAN GO TO BED NOW, WE'RE LEAVING AT ONCE.

RIGHT, ME HEARTIES, WE'RE FAR ENOUGH FROM SHORE NOW. LET'S PLUCK OUR THREE PIGEONS.

THEY'RE ASLEEP. GOOD! EXCELLENT, EX...

CAP'N! HELP! CAP'N!

WHAT?

SSSH! L...LOOK! THE GAU... THE GAU-GAU...

LOOK ON THIS JUST AS A MATTER OF COURSE, LADS! AFTER ALL, THEY DIDN'T WAKE UP, THERE'S ALWAYS THAT!

ERRARE HUMANUM EST.

NEXT MORNING...

?

NO ONE AROUND! THEY'VE ABANDONED SHIP!

WELL, NEVER MIND. JUDGING BY THE SUN, WE'RE ON THE RIGHT COURSE FOR CORSICA.

BUT I'M HUNGRY!

SNIFF, SNIFF.

COME ON, THEN! VERMICELLIX GAVE ME A CORSICAN CHEESE. YOU'LL FIND IT'S QUITE SOMETHING!

TAKE A SNIFF AT THAT, FRIENDS!

I...I THINK I'LL JUST GO AND LIE DOWN...

FLICK!

HOWL! HOWL! HOWL!

AH, THAT AROMA...

SNIFF! SNIFF!

SUCH A DELICATE, SUBTLE AROMA, CALLING TO MIND THYME AND ALMOND TREES, FIG TREES, CHESTNUT TREES... AND THEN AGAIN, THE FAINTEST HINT OF PINES, A TOUCH OF TARRAGON, A SUGGESTION OF ROSEMARY AND LAVENDER... AH, MY FRIENDS, THAT AROMA...

...IS THE ESSENCE OF CORSICA!

CORSICA!

THESE CORSICANS ARE CRAZY!

OH, COME ON, LET'S FOLLOW HIM.

TAP! TAP! TAP!

SPLASH!

SPLASH!

SPLASH!

SMELL THAT WATER! THAT MARVELLOUS SCENT OF LOBSTER, SEA URCHIN AND SHRIMP!

PERSONALLY, I THINK IT SMELLS OF ROMANS... ISN'T THAT A FORTIFIED ROMAN CAMP OVER THERE?

YES, THERE ARE CAMPS ALL ROUND THE SHORES OF THE ISLANDS. IT'S WHEN THEY TRY GETTING INTO THE MAQUIS IN THE INTERIOR THE ROMANS HAVE PROBLEMS.

BUT DON'T WORRY. THE ROMANS WHO GET SENT HERE ARE USUALLY A POOR LOT, POSTED TO CORSICA BY WAY OF PUNISHMENT. IT'S ONLY THE PRAETOR WHO KEEPS A FEW CRACK TROOPS AT ALERIA.

SEE THAT? WE'D BETTER LET THE CENTURION KNOW!

YEAH... ANYWAY, DON'T LET'S HANG AROUND HERE.

HURRY UP, CAN'T YOU?

TAKE IT EASY, NOW... JUST TAKE IT EASY!

YOU'RE NEW HERE, SO TAKE IT VERY, VERY EASY AND I'LL EXPLAIN THINGS.

THE SAND! TAKE A SNIFF AT THIS SAND!

WOULDN'T THERE BE ANY WAY OF GETTING A SNIFF OF A BOAR?

YOU'RE RIGHT! COME ON! WE'LL GO UP THE MOUNTAIN TO MY VILLAGE.

SOON AFTERWARDS...

AVE, CENTURION! WE HAVE OBSERVED THREE MEN ABANDONING THEIR SHIP IN ORDER TO MAKE AN ILLEGAL ENTRY INTO CORSICA.

HOW LONG AGO?

WELL, AS LONG AS IT TOOK US TO GET BACK HERE, AND MY CALIGAE ARE KILLING ME, SO WE DIDN'T GO VERY FAST.

RIGHT, LET'S TAKE A LOOK AT THIS SHIP.

SCRATCH! SCRATCH!

THE SHIP? BUT I'D HAVE THOUGHT IT WAS THE MEN WHO...

YOU MAY BE THE ONE VOLUNTEER IN THIS GARRISON, COURTINGDISASTUS, BUT YOU'RE GETTING ME DOWN! WE'RE GOING TO LOOK AT THAT SHIP AND WRITE A REPORT!

SOON AFTERWARDS

SURE ENOUGH, THE SHIP'S ABANDONED. RIGHT, BACK WE GO TO WRITE THE REPORT.

CENTURION, THERE'S A BOAT FULL OF PEOPLE NOT FAR OFF!

ONE REPORT AT A TIME! WE'LL COME BACK TOMORROW AND WRITE A REPORT ON THIS BOAT OF YOURS IF IT'S STILL AROUND.

SOME ROMANS JUST LEAVING OUR SHIP... IT LOOKS DESERTED. WE CAN TAKE IT BACK, ME HEARTIES!

THIS WHOLE THING SMELLS A BIT...

THEY COULD STILL BE HIDDEN ON BOARD. FELIX QUI POTUIT RERUM COGNOSCERE CAUSAS, IF YOU'LL PARDON MY LATIN.

22

RIGHT, THERE'S NOTHING LEFT FOR US TO DO HERE. WE'RE OFF.

WHAT DO YOU MEAN, WE'RE OFF? WHAT ABOUT THIS?

WELL, WHAT ABOUT IT? A SHIP ARRIVES, THREE CHARACTERS DIVE INTO THE SEA, THE SHIP'S ABANDONED, IT BLOWS UP, ANOTHER SET OF CHARACTERS COME SWIMMING ASHORE...

MERE COMMONPLACE. HARDLY WORTH WRITING A REPORT AT ALL.

I DISAGREE, CENTURION. WE OUGHT TO WARN PRAETOR PERFIDIUS AT ALERIA!

BY JUPITER AND MERCURY! ARE YOU LOOKING FOR TROUBLE, COURTINGDISASTUS? WELL, YOU CAN HAVE IT! YOU CAN ESCORT THESE IDIOTS TO ALERIA!

MEANWHILE...

MY VILLAGE IS QUITE CLOSE.

IS HE FROM YOUR VILLAGE?

YES, THAT'S LETHARGIX OUR DRUID. HE'S BUSY GATHERING MISTLETOE.

THAT'S THE WAY HE GATHERS MISTLETOE?

YES, HE'S WAITING FOR IT TO FALL OFF THE TREE.

TOC! TOC! TOC! TOC!

OH, LOOK! TAME BOARS!

NO, THOSE ARE WILD PIGS.

ISN'T THAT LITTLE BONEYWASA-WARRIORWAYAYIX WHO WENT TO THE CONTINENT?

YES. I KNEW THEY WOULDN'T WANT TO KEEP HIM.

THE OTHERS AREN'T LOCALS. LOOK AT THAT DOG, HE'S NO BIGGER THAN A BLACKBIRD.

HE DOESN'T GET ENOUGH SIESTA.

CHIEF BONEYWASAWARRIORWAYAYIX! YOU'RE BACK!

PLEASED TO SEE YOU, CARFERRIX.

TO THINK WE WERE JUST ABOUT TO HOLD ELECTIONS FOR A NEW CHIEF. THE BALLOT BOXES ARE ALREADY FULL.

YOU MEAN THE BALLOT BOXES ARE FULL BEFORE THE ELECTION'S HELD?

YES, BUT WE THROW THEM INTO THE SEA WITHOUT OPENING THEM, AND THEN THE STRONGEST MAN WINS. IT'S AN OLD CORSICAN CUSTOM.

MEET ASTERIX, OBELIX AND DOGMATIX. THEY'VE COME TO SEE HOW WE CORSICANS DEAL WITH THE ROMANS.

WHY NOT COME AND HAVE SOME WILD PIG AT MY PLACE?

25

LOOK, NO BIGGER THAN A CHESTNUT, BUT HE EATS AS IF HIS SIESTA DEPENDED ON IT!

SCRUNCH! SCRUNCH!

FLICK! FLICK!

WELL, HOW ARE THINGS GOING?

THE WAREHOUSES OF ALERIA ARE FULL OF THE LOOT PRAETOR PERFIDIUS HAS TAKEN. THERE ISN'T MUCH TIME LEFT, THE PRAETOR WILL SOON BE RECALLED TO ROME.

THEN WHY NOT ATTACK NOW?

ALERIA IS WELL DEFENDED. WE NEED TIME TO SUMMON EVERYONE FROM THE OTHER VILLAGES. THAT'S WHAT I WAS DOING WHEN I WAS CAPTURED IN OLABELLAMARGARITIX'S VILLAGE.

CRRiiii!

OLABELLA-MARGARITIX?

MY CLAN AND OLABELLAMARGARITIX'S CLAN HAVE A VENDETTA GOING, BUT I NEVER THOUGHT HE'D BETRAY ME TO THE ROMANS.

THERE'S NO PROOF HE DID...

THE OLABELLAMARGARITIX CLAN ARE CAPABLE OF ANYTHING!

WHAT'S THE VENDETTA ABOUT?

NO ONE'S TOO SURE ANY MORE...

THE OLD FOLK SAY BONEYWASAWARRIORWAYAYiX'S GREAT-UNCLE MARRIED A GIRL FROM THE VIOLONCELLiX CLAN, AND A COUSiN BY MARRIAGE OF ONE OF OLABELLAMARGARITIX'S GRAND-FATHERS WAS IN LOVE WITH HER...

BUT OTHERS SAY IT WAS BECAUSE OF A DONKEY WHICH OLABELLAMARGARITIX'S GREAT-GRANDFATHER REFUSED TO PAY FOR WHEN HE GOT HIM FROM THE BROTHER-IN-LAW OF A CLOSE FRIEND OF THE BONEYWASAWARRIORWAYAYiX CLAN, CLAIMING THAT HE WAS LAME (THE DONKEY, NOT THE BONEYWASAWARRIORWAYAYiXES' FRIEND'S BROTHER-IN-LAW)...

...ANYWAY, IT'S VERY SERIOUS.

TAP! TAP! TAP!

?

ALERIA...

A LEGIONARY TO SEE YOU, O PRAETOR PERFIDIUS. HE SAYS HE HAS IMPORTANT INFORMATION.

SHOW HIM IN.

AVE, PRAETOR! THIS MAN WANTS TO SPIN YOU A YARN.

NO, I DON'T! I'M AN HONEST SAILOR WORKING THE MASSILIA-CORSICA CROSSING...

I TOOK THREE PASSENGERS ON BOARD, AND BEFORE THEY DISAPPEARED THEY BLEW UP MY SHIP WITH AN INFERNAL DEVICE IN THE FORM OF A CHEESE...

A CORSICAN CHEESE?

ANYWAY, ONE OF THE PASSENGERS WAS CORSICAN... THEY CALLED HIM BONEYWASAWARRIOR POMTIDDLYPOM.

WAYAYIX?!

YES, THAT'S RIGHT. NOT POMTIDDLYPOM, WAYAYIX. THERE WERE TWO GAULS WITH HIM, TWO REAL THREATS TO SHIPPING WHO...

WHERE DID THEY GO?

I SAW THEM MAKE OFF INLAND, TOWARDS THE MOUNTAINS. I REQUEST THE HONOUR OF PARTICIPATING IN THE SEARCH IF THESE MEN ARE OUTLAWS.

OUTLAWS? BONEYWASAWARRIORWAYAYIX IS THE WORST OF BANDITS! HE'S AFTER CAESAR'S TAXES. I'D EXILED HIM... WE MUST CAPTURE HIM!

O PRAETOR, I WILL RECAPTURE BONEYWASAWARRIORHEYNONNYNO!

WAYAYIX.

YOU'RE COURTING DISASTUS...

YES, I VOLUNTEERED TO COME TO CORSICA. I HEARD CHANCES OF PROMOTION WERE GOOD.

RIGHT! I APPOINT YOU LEADER OF THE PATROL WHICH IS GOING AFTER THE BANDIT. HIS VILLAGE IS THE FIRST ON THE LEFT AS YOU GO UP THE VALLEY.

I'LL NEED SOME MEN.

EASY! TRUMPETER, BLOW THE CALL TO FETCH 'EM...

?

COME TO THE COOKHOUSE DOOR, BOYS!!!

EXCELLENT! THE FIRST TEN MEN HAVE VOLUNTEERED TO GO AND RECAPTURE BONEYWASAWARRIORWAYAYIX!

I TOLD YOU, YOU FOOL, DIDN'T I? WE'D ONLY JUST HAD A MEAL!

YOU WERE RIGHT... I HADN'T EVEN FINISHED EATING.

I'LL BRING BACK THE BANDIT, PRAETOR. AVE!

CLAC!

FORWARD MARCH, MEN!

I DOUBT IF YOU WILL BRING HIM BACK, YOU POOR FOOL... I SHALL HAVE TO PUT THE LOOT SOMEWHERE SAFE...

CAESAR WARNED ME... IF I DIDN'T BRING PLENTY OF LOOT BACK TO ROME, HE'D SEND ME TO GAUL... APPARENTLY THERE'S A VILLAGE THERE WHOSE PEOPLE ARE EVEN WORSE THAN THE CORSICANS... AND THEY HAVE NOTHING BUT FISH TO BE LOOTED...

AND I'VE HEARD IT ISN'T ALWAYS FRESH, EITHER.

APPARENTLY HE VOLUNTEERED TO COME TO CORSICA!

WE'VE GOT A MADMAN IN CHARGE, ON TOP OF IT ALL!

I WAS COURT-MARTIALLED BACK IN ROME, GIVEN A CHOICE OF THE CIRCUS OR CORSICA... YOU KNOW WHAT THE ARMY'S LIKE, YOU ONLY HAVE TO ASK FOR ONE THING TO GET THE OPPOSITE.

THERE WAS THIS OPTIO GOT ME DRUNK IN A TAVERN IN GENUA... WHEN I WOKE UP I WAS HERE. I'VE NEVER TOUCHED A DROP SINCE.

SILENCE IN THE RANKS! WE MUST TAKE THE BANDIT BY SURPRISE!

BY SURPRISE! DON'T MAKE ME LAUGH.

HEE HAW! HEE HAW!

FURTHER OFF...

HEE HAW! HEE HAW!

OINK! OINK!

POC!

OINK! OINK!

GO TO THE VILLAGE, WILL YOU, AND TELL THEM THERE'S A PATROL OF ELEVEN ROMANS COMING THIS WAY.

CAN'T EVEN FISH IN PEACE THESE DAYS. EVERY SIX MONTHS IT'S THE SAME OLD STORY.

CHIPOLATA! POUR US SOME MORE WINE!

CARFERRIX!

COMING!

THANK YOU.

TELL YOUR FRIEND TO WATCH OUT. CARFERRIX DOESN'T LIKE PEOPLE BEING DISRESPECTFUL TO HIS SISTER.

BUT HE DIDN'T DO ANYTHING DISRESPECTFUL.

YES, HE DID. HE SPOKE TO HER. HE SMILED, TOO. SO WATCH OUT!

!?!

BONEYWASAWARRIORWAYAYIX, THERE ARE SOME ROMANS COMING.

RIGHT! WE'LL BE OFF TO THE MAQUIS.

THE MAQUIS?

YES. THE ROMANS WILL GET LOST THERE, YOU WAIT AND SEE.

HE CERTAINLY WON'T!

I TAKE NO FURTHER INTEREST IN THE MATTER.

SAME HERE. IT'S NONE OF MY BUSINESS.

GET READY TO PICK HIM UP, HE WON'T BE EXPECTING THIS!

SEE THAT? THE VILLAGE IS PEACEFUL... WE'LL START WITH THE FIRST HOUSE, OVER THERE...

THEIR LEADER MUST BE NEW.

HE REMINDS ME OF SALAMIX, WHO FELL OUT OF A CHESTNUT TREE AND LANDED ON HIS HEAD.

I HEARD HE JOINED THE ROMAN ARMY AFTER THAT.

YES, HE'D GONE SO HALF-WITTED YOU HAD TIME TO STONE HIS DONKEY TO DEATH WITH RIPE FIGS BEFORE YOU COULD GET THROUGH TO HIM.

26

30

THUMP!
THUMP!
THUMP!

AVE!

I HAVE A WARRANT TO SEARCH, IN THE NAME OF PRAETOR PERFIDIUS, REPRESENTATIVE OF JULIUS CAESAR IN CORSICA!

CHIPOLATA, GET BACK INTO THE HOUSE.

...

!

ER... WELL, I WAS SAYING AVE, AND IN THE NAME OF PRAETOR PERFIDIUS, REPRESENTATIVE OF JULIUS CAESAR...

27A

GLOP!

YOU SPOKE TO MY SISTER.

I DID?... I DIDN'T REALISE...

I DON'T LIKE PEOPLE SPEAKING TO MY SISTER.

FLICK!
FLICK!

BETTER WATCH OUT, MATES.

27B

31

33

WE'RE GOING BACK TO MAKE OUR REPORT TO PRAETOR PERFIDIUS, AND THEN WE'LL BE BACK IN FORCE TO PICK UP THESE BANDITS!

YOU IDIOT, WE'VE GOT TO FIND OUT HOW TO GET BACK FIRST!

LET'S HOLD HANDS, BOYS.

BY JUPITER, THIS PLACE IS SWARMING WITH PIGS!

A ROMAN ROAD! **OH, FOR A ROMAN ROAD!**

GROÏNK

GROÏNK

ON TOP OF THE MOUNTAIN...

WELL, IF YOU'D PICKED UP A FEW YOURSELF I WOULDN'T HAVE TO LEND YOU SOME OF MINE.

YOU PIG!

WE'LL SHELTER IN THIS CAVE.

NOW ALL WE HAVE TO DO IS WAIT FOR THE REPRESENTATIVES OF THE OTHER CLANS, AND THEN WE ORGANISE OUR ATTACK ON ALERIA. THE PEOPLE OF MY VILLAGE HAVE SENT THEM WORD.

LET'S HOPE THE PRAETOR DOESN'T HAVE TIME TO GET HIS LOOT TO SAFETY!

SCRUNCH! SCRUNCH!

ANYWAY, WE LIKE THE MAQUIS, DOGMATIX AND ME. IT'S FULL OF PIGS AND ROMANS!

GRF!

IN THE PRAETOR'S OFFICE IN ALERIA...

THE FACT THAT YOU ARE THE ONLY NATIVE CORSICAN LEGIONARY MAKES YOU IDEAL FOR THIS SECRET MISSION. SERVE ME WELL AND YOU WON'T REGRET IT, SALAMIX!

YEAH, SURE!

30

THE CORSICANS ARE GOING TO ATTACK ALERIA AND RAID THE WAREHOUSES...

YEAH?

SO, VERY DISCREETLY, YOU ARE GOING TO MOVE THE CONTENTS OF THE WAREHOUSES AND GET THEM ON BOARD THE BIG GALLEY OUT IN THE HARBOUR...

THE BIG GALLEY, YEAH...

FOR THIS OPERATION YOU WILL EMPLOY THE CORSICAN PRISONERS NOW BUILDING THE ROMAN ROAD...

THE ROMAN ROAD, YEAH...

AS A REWARD FOR THEIR WORK, THE CORSICAN PRISONERS WILL BE SET FREE... BUT BE CAREFUL! I DON'T WANT THE GARRISON TO GET WIND OF THIS!

YOU DON'T?

NO, BECAUSE ONCE THE GALLEY IS LOADED UP WE'LL GO ABOARD OURSELVES, AND SAIL AWAY FROM CORSICA, LEAVING THE GARRISON BEHIND TO DEFEND THE EMPTY WAREHOUSES! HA, HA, HA!

HA, HA, HA!

YOU'LL HAVE TO WORK ALL NIGHT... NOW, IS THAT ALL QUITE CLEAR?

ER...

NO.

NEVER MIND! DO JUST AS I SAY, AND YOU'LL COME BACK TO ROME WITH ME, BE RICH AND RESPECTED ...

YEAH?

THE ROMAN ROAD BEING BUILT BETWEEN ALERIA AND MARIANA.... THE ROADWORKS HAVE BEEN IN PROGRESS FOR THREE YEARS...

HEY... I'VE GOT WORK FOR YOU.

NOT JUST A TRAITOR, FOUL-MOUTHED TOO!

THAT NIGHT, ON BOARD A GALLEY IN THE PORT OF ALERIA...

...AND ONCE THE SHIP IS LOADED UP, YOU WILL SAIL HER TO ROME. I SHALL BE ON BOARD WITH SALAMIX, WE'LL BE GETTING RID OF HIM DURING THE VOYAGE...

IT ALL HAS TO BE DONE TONIGHT... THE GARRISON MUSTN'T KNOW I'M ABANDONING THEM. THEY WILL FIGHT, AND THUS COVER MY ESCAPE...

AND AFTERWARDS YOU'LL GIVE US THE SHIP AND SET US FREE? THAT'S A PROMISE?

WHAT REASON CAN YOU HAVE TO DOUBT MY GOOD FAITH?

MEANWHILE...

RIGHT, GET WORKING. YOU MUST CARRY ALL THIS ON BOARD THE GALLEY.

TWENTY MINUTES LATER...

WHERE DO I PUT THIS?

AT THIS RATE IT'S GOING TO TAKE YEARS! AND WE HAVE TO STOP WORK AT DAYBREAK BECAUSE OF THE GARRISON!

THERE'S NO HURRY, BOYS. WE'VE GOT YEARS TO FINISH THE JOB, AND WE DON'T NEED TO DO ANYTHING DURING THE DAY.

I'VE GOT A COUSIN WHO HAS A JOB LIKE THAT, IN THE CIVIL SERVICE IN MASSILIA.

LOOKS LIKE THE ROMANS WILL FIND OUR LADS TOUGH NUTS TO CRACK!

THAT'S A HOARY OLD CORSICAN CHESTNUT! LET'S GO AND SEE HOW THE YOUNG 'UNS COPE... DON'T SUPPOSE THEY'RE UP TO MUCH.

SHALL WE TAKE THE TREE-TRUNK?

YOU'RE NUTTY, TORTELLINIX! WE'LL ASK THE YOUNG 'UNS TO CUT ONE DOWN FOR US WHEN WE GET THERE.

COMING FROM THE VILLAGES, THE MOUNTAINS AND THE MAQUIS, THE CORSICANS MAKE FOR THE BLEAK PLAIN OF ALERIA...

WHAT A LOT OF THEM!

YES, WE'RE FULL OF CLAN FEELING.

34

SEE THAT COLUMN OVER THERE? THOSE ARE THE CORSICANS WHOSE CHIEF MARRIED INTO A CALEDONIAN CLAN...

GROINNK-

GROINNK-

GROINNK!

GROINNK!

GROINNK!

THE CLAN OF MACARONIX.

34

RAISE THE ALARM! RAISE THE ALARM! CORSICANS! MASSES OF CORSICANS OUTSIDE THE TOWN!

WELL, WELL! AND I THOUGHT THE CORSICANS WEREN'T GOING TO ATTACK?

WE'LL DISCUSS ALL THAT LATER! WE MUST MAKE A SORTIE OR THEY'LL FORCE THEIR WAY IN!

RIGHT, BUT YOU'RE COMING WITH US!

WE WANT TO BE SURE YOU'LL STAY TILL THE END OF THE BATTLE.

THIS IS MUTINY! YOU CAN'T FORCE YOUR LEADER TO LEAD THE WAY!

AH! ABOUT TIME TOO.

THESE THINGS NEVER START PUNCTUALLY.

I REMEMBER THE DAYS WHEN IT WAS A CONTINUOUS PERFORMANCE.

I DIDN'T KNOW THE PRAETOR WAS IN THE ACT TOO.

WHO... WHO ARE THOSE TWO?

I DON'T KNOW, BUT I'M NOT TOO KEEN ON BEING IN THE FRONT LINE!

CLAP CLAP CLAP CLAPCLAPCLAPCLAP!

I BROUGHT THEM TO SHOW THEM WHAT WE CAN DO, AND NOW THEY'RE GIVING US A LESSON! AND THEY'RE FROM THE CONTINENT TOO!

LET'S GO! WE CAN SORT IT ALL OUT LATER!

37

WELL, HERE THEY COME AFTER ALL.

THESE YOUNG FOLK HAVE NO IDEA OF PUNCTUALITY.

ISN'T THAT LITTLE SALAMIX OUT AHEAD OF THE REST?

SO IT IS! I GET THE IMPRESSION HE'S STILL A BIT EMPTY-HEADED.

PAF!

!?

TCHONK!

WHAT... WHAT AM I DOING HERE?

YOU'RE A TRAITOR!

A TRAITOR? ME? JUST REPEAT THAT!

YOU CAN FIGHT LATER. WE'VE GOT A BATTLE FIRST.

BATTLE? WHO WITH?

WITH THE ROMANS, OF COURSE!

THE ROMANS? CHARGE! CHARGE!

AFTER A BRIEF BUT VIOLENT EPISODE...

WELL, DO WE CAST OFF?

NO POINT CASTING PEARLS BEFORE SWINE NOW...

IS THAT MEANT TO HAVE US IN STITCHES? CAP'N, WITH DUE RESPECT, YOU'RE A SILLY KNIT.

PRAETOR, WE WILL ALLOW YOU AND YOUR MEN TO LIVE, SO THAT YOU CAN TELL CAESAR WHAT YOU HAVE SEEN!

WE SHALL RECOVER ALL YOU HAVE STOLEN FROM YOUR WAREHOUSES, AND LET THAT BE A LESSON TO YOUR MASTER!

JULIUS CAESAR WILL HAVE HIS REVENGE!

TELL CAESAR THAT, NO MATTER WHAT HIS AMBITIONS, HE WILL NEVER RULE US...

THE PEOPLE OF CORSICA WILL NEVER ACCEPT AN EMPEROR UNLESS HE IS A CORSICAN HIMSELF! GO!

THAT'S RIGHT! OINK!

THREE CHEERS!

NOW, HOW ABOUT A FEW EXPLANATIONS, BONEYWASAWARRIORWAYAYIX?

YES, OLABELLAMARGARITIX!

WHY DID YOU ACCUSE ME OF BETRAYING YOU TO THE ROMANS?

YOU WERE THE ONLY PERSON WHO KNEW I HAD COME TO YOUR VILLAGE... AND THEN THE ROMANS CAME ALONG DURING MY SIESTA.

FLICK! FLICK!

WE DIDN'T KNOW THEY WERE COMING. WE JUST TOOK ADVANTAGE OF YOUR SIESTA TO GO AND TAKE PROVISIONS TO COUSIN RIGATONIX WHO'S BEEN HIDING IN THE MAQUIS FOR THIRTY YEARS OVER THAT BUSINESS OF LASAGNIX'S GREAT-AUNT.

I REMEMBER! THE PRAETOR DIDN'T GET A TIP-OFF FROM OLABELLAMARGARITIX. HE SIMPLY HAD YOU FOLLOWED, AND WHEN OLABELLAMARGARITIX AND HIS MEN WENT OFF, HE TOOK HIS CHANCE TO CAPTURE YOU.

MAYBE... BUT THAT DOESN'T SETTLE THE BUSINESS OF YOUR GREAT-GRANDFATHER WHO WOULDN'T PAY FOR THE DONKEY WHICH...

STOP IT.

THAT'S QUITE ENOUGH PAST HISTORY!

YOU'VE BEEN FIGHTING TOGETHER AGAINST YOUR OPPRESSOR, AND YOU'LL HAVE TO FIGHT AGAIN IF YOU'RE TO REMAIN FREE, SO SHAKE HANDS!

CREAK-CREAK!

HURRAH FOR BONEYWASAWARRIORWAYAYIX!

HURRAH FOR OLABELLAMARGARITIX!

HURRAH FOR ASTERIX!

LET'S HAVE A PARTY!

OINK!

BEATING THE ROMANS IS NOTHING, BUT SETTLING A VENDETTA BETWEEN TWO CLANS IS AN AMAZING FEAT!

SUCH POINTLESS FEUDS WILL NEVER EXIST IN CORSICA AGAIN!

GOOD... AND NOW WE MUST BE GETTING HOME TO GAUL, BONEYWASA-WARRIORWAYAYIX.

WHAT WOULD YOU LIKE AS A PRESENT FROM CORSICA?

THAT DEAR LITTLE DOG.

HEY, OLABELLA-MARGARITIX!

?

WE AND COUSIN LASAGNIX WOULD LIKE TO KNOW WHERE YOUR COUSIN RIGATONIX IS. WE WANT A WORD WITH HIM.

I'M NOT SAYING, SPAGHETTIX.

YOU'LL BE SORRY FOR THIS, OLABELLAMARGA-RITIX.

WE MAY NOTE IN PASSING THAT, AS A RESULT OF THIS RATHER COMPLICATED MATTER, ONE OF THE DESCENDANTS OF THE OLABELLAMARGARITIX CLAN WAS FOUND LAST YEAR BY THE POLICE, HIDING IN THE MAQUIS BEHIND A MOTEL.

43

47

HERE THEY COME! **THEY'RE BACK!**

WELL, BOYS, WAS IT NICE IN CORSICA?

IT WAS FINE. NICE PLACE THEY'VE GOT THERE. MOUNTAINS, FORESTS, MOUNTAIN STREAMS, MAQUIS...

AND SOME INTERESTING ROMAN REMAINS, DATING FROM THE TIME OF OUR VISIT.

AND THERE WERE SOME VERY NICE PIGS, AND DOGMATIX MADE LOTS OF FRIENDS...

DIDN'T YOU, DOGMATIX?

AS USUAL, OUR FRIENDS' RETURN IS THE EXCUSE FOR A BANQUET HELD UNDER THE STARS... AND WE MAY NOTE THAT EACH OF THEIR JOURNEYS ENRICHES THE TRAVELLERS' EXPERIENCE, SINCE THEY ADOPT SOME OF THE MORE PLEASANT CUSTOMS OF THE COUNTRIES THEY HAVE VISITED.

THE END

UDERZO & GOSCINNY
4.73

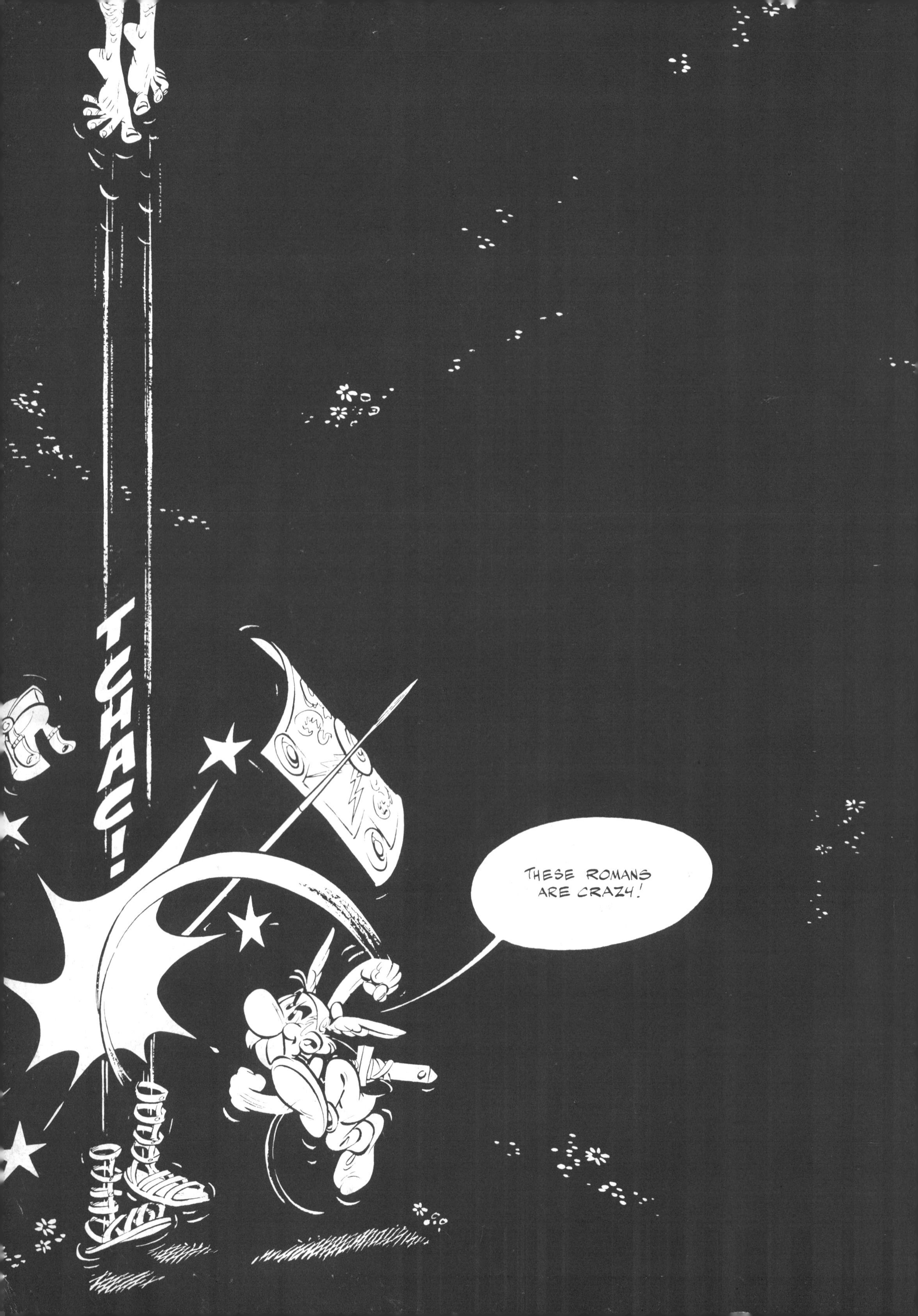
THACI!
THESE ROMANS ARE CRAZY!